THIS CANDLEWICK BOOK BELONGS TO:

To Rhea Zaib
Have a fun, safe trip
to India. Stop by and
see us in September!

Love,
Mrs. Hanson

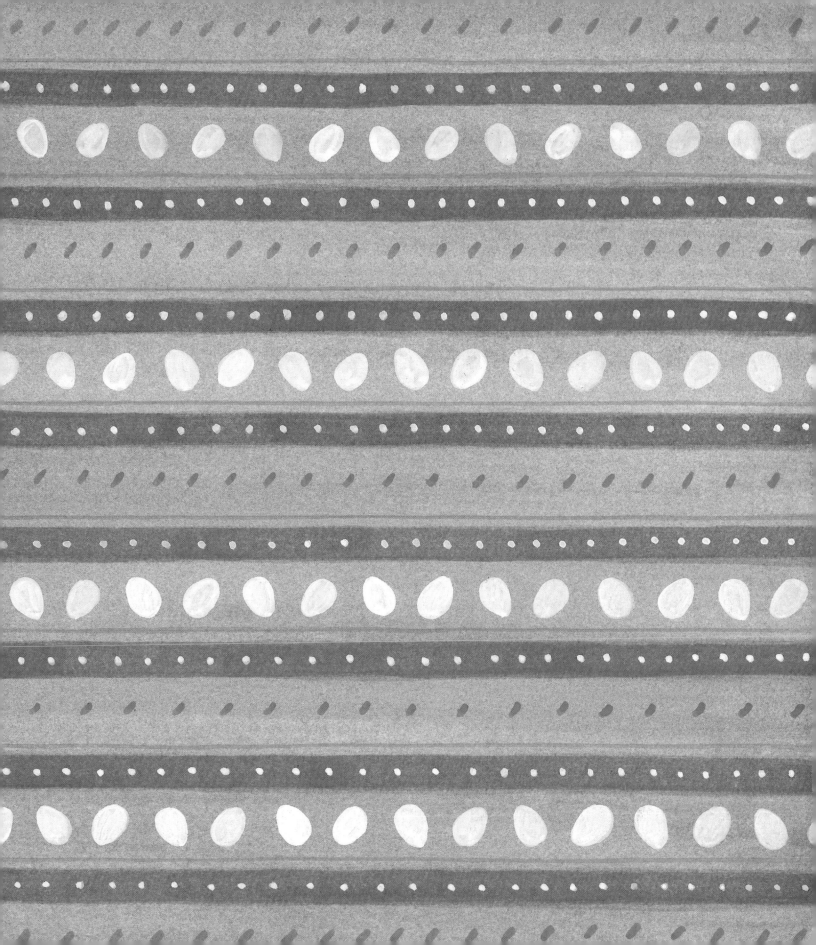

In Memory of
Humpty Dumpty

First paperback edition 1996

The Library of Congress has cataloged the hardcover edition as follows:

Imai, Miko, 1963–
Little Lumpty / Miko Imai. — 1st ed.
Summary: Many years after Humpty Dumpty fell,
another curious and daring fellow discovers the dangerous
attraction of that high brick wall.
ISBN 1-56402-233-1 (hardcover)
[1. Eggs—Fiction.]   I. Title.
PZ7. I333Li   1993
[E]—dc20   93-22358
ISBN 1-56402-829-1 (paperback)

2 4 6 8 10 9 7 5 3

Printed in Hong Kong

This book was typeset in Stone Informal.
The pictures were done in gouache.

Candlewick Press
2067 Massachusetts Avenue
Cambridge, Massachusetts 02140

LITTLE LUMPTY

Miko Imai

CANDLEWICK PRESS

CAMBRIDGE, MASSACHUSETTS

In the little town of Dumpty there was a high wall.
Humpty Dumpty had fallen from it long, long ago.
But people still remembered him.

Every day children played by the wall and sang,
"Humpty Dumpty sat on the wall.
Humpty Dumpty had a great fall."

Little Lumpty loved the wall and always
dreamed about climbing to the top.

"Don't ever do that," Lumpty's mother said.
"Remember, all the king's horses and all the king's men
couldn't put Humpty Dumpty together again."

But Lumpty couldn't stop thinking about the wall.

One day on his way home from school, he found
a long ladder and dragged it over there.

He climbed up …
and up … and up.

At last he reached the top. "Oh, there's my house!

And there's my school! I can almost touch the clouds!"

Lumpty was so happy that he danced along like a tightrope walker.

"If only my friends could see me now!"

But then Lumpty looked down. IT WAS A BIG

MISTAKE. His legs began to shake and tremble.

"Oh, no! I don't think I can get back to the ladder."

"What if I'm not home by dinnertime?"

It was getting dark and the birds were flying home
to their nests, but still Lumpty could not move.
Suddenly he remembered Humpty Dumpty's great fall.

"Help! Help!" Lumpty screamed.

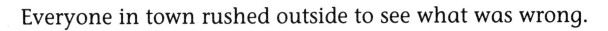

Everyone in town rushed outside to see what was wrong.

"How can we save him?" asked an old man.
"We need a big blanket!" said Lumpty's mother,
and she ran home to get one.

They stretched it out at the bottom of the wall.
"Jump, Lumpty, jump!
  Jump, Lumpty, jump!"

Lumpty took a deep breath and
threw himself into the dark night air.

He bounced once,

twice,

three times,

and then came safely to rest on the blanket.

"Mommy, I'm sorry. I just had to see
what it would be like on top."

He was so glad to be home.

"But I still love that wall," he whispered to the moon just before he fell asleep.

MIKO IMAI was born in Niigata, Japan, in 1963. A graduate of Musachino Art University and the Rhode Island School of Design, she worked as a textile designer before launching her career as a freelance illustrator. Rescuing Humpty Dumpty from his famous fall has long been a dream of hers. Finding that quite impossible, she created Little Lumpty, whom she *could* save. The author-illustrator of *Lilly's Secret* and *Sebastian's Trumpet*, and the illustrator of *Wuzzy Takes Off*, by Robin and Helen Lester, Miko Imai lives in Lexington, Massachusetts.